I0683369

Reprint Publishing

For People Who Go For Originals.

www.reprintpublishing.com

POTTED FICTION

POTTED FICTION

Being a series of extracts
from
The·World's·Best·Sellers

PUT·UP·IN·THIN·SLICES
FOR·HURRIED·CONSUMERS

THE UNITED STATES LITERARY CANNING Co.

EDITED BY
JOHN KENDRICK BANGS

NEW YORK
Doubleday, Page & Co.
1908.

FOREWORD

THIS library of Condensed Best Sellers is designed to meet the literary needs of those who have troubles of their own so numerous that they have not much spare time to devote to the trials and tribulations of the heroes and heroines of the hour. It is the purpose of THE UNITED STATES LITERARY CANNING COMPANY, of Pennsylvania, to put up in small packages, of which this is a sample, the most talked of literary products of our best, if not most famous, authors, in such convenient form that they may be carried in a vest pocket, or a vanity bag, to be consumed as opportunity presents on trolley-cars, between courses at quick lunch counters, between rubbers at bridge parties, or in those restful hours which the consumer may be called upon to endure at lectures, during after-dinner speeches of unusual length, or between the acts of current dramas and comic operas. The company has endeavoured to provide in this small compass a concentrated literary extract that shall have all the pungent flavour, and nourishing qualities of the original work on the hoof. The extracts are all prepared in laboratories especially built for the purpose, the apartments being porcelain lined, the floors of tiled concrete, on tables made of glass, by sterilised condensers using antiseptic vaccine quills instead of pens, the ink having been parboiled and filtered according to the very latest hygienic principles before use. The company will give $10,000 in its own third deferred sixth mortgage debenture certificates, issue of 1908 and maturing in 3797, to any consumer finding the slightest trace of formaldehyde, peroxide, jimmiehyde, or subway dust in any of its preparations, and especially warns its patrons against imitations. Every can of POTTED FICTION issued by this company has the initials U. S. L. C. C. blown in the label by a special blower hired for the purpose at enormous expense.

We call attention to the following testimonials all of which were unsolicited:

FROM THE MAYOR OF SQUANTUMVILLE, SOUTH DAKOTA.

Since using six cans of your POTTED FICTION our Common Council has closed the Carnegie Library as superfluous.

FROM PROFESSOR SLANGWHANGER, R. F. D., HOBOKUS BUSINESS COLLEGE.

We are now using your POTTED FICTION as a text-book in our literary courses, and many of our football players have learned to read for the express purpose of tasting the delights of your preparation.

FROM HIRAM BRIGGS, FOR TWENTY YEARS A SUFFERER FROM INSOMNIA.

Your literary capsules have just arrived, and they are a revelation. I took two upon retiring last night, and have not waked up since. Many thanks.

FROM A PETITION SIGNED BY TWO HUNDRED MEMBERS OF CONGRESS.

Your POTTED FICTION has passed to its third reading and will be adopted before adjournment as the official literature of the country. Can you not enlarge the scope of your enterprise so as to include the President's Messages?

FROM ANDREW ROCKERNEGIE, CAPITALIST, AND PHILAN-THROPIST

Please send me eight million cans of your POTTED FICTION I want twenty copies in every Rockernegie Library in the land, and enclose a blank cheque signed to be filled in for whatever sum you deem proper.

The above testimonials selected from a million received during the past week, and entirely at random, speak for themselves. Can you afford to be without such an article? Probably not, but you will have to if you do not get your order in at once, as the demand is increasing in such proportions that we are seriously thinking of retiring from business on the profits already in hand.

THE UNITED STATES LITERARY CANNING COMPANY,

Per Wilberforce Jenkins, President.

CONTENTS

POTTED FICTION

POTTED FICTION

ROLLO IN THE METROLOPUS

By DOPETON HOTAIR

CHAPTER I

WHEN Rollo descended from the train at Jersey City he was surprised to find a crimson carpet laid on the station platform, that stretched as far as the eye could reach, on each side of which, in perfect alignment, stood all the prominent members of New York society, who had come there on the invitation of his brother Monty to welcome him to their city.

"Why, look who's here," cried a familiar voice, and Rollo, turning to see who the speaker might be, was delighted to find himself face to face with his brother, whom he had not seen since, penniless, he had left home three weeks before to make his fortune in New York. The brothers shook hands cordially.

"Who are all these people?" asked Rollo, gazing down the long line of tired faces.

"They are the smart set. They may not look smart, but they are," returned Monty. "But never mind them now — where are your trunk cheques?"

"I haven't brought any trunks," returned Rollo. "I have only a change of neckties in my pocket. If you will remember, Monty, you took the family underclothing and our hereditary dress suit with you when you left home."

"So I did," said the latter, "but that is no reason why you should not have brought a lot of trunks with you. If you want to make any kind of an impression in polite circles in this burg you've got to have a lot of baggage when you travel. I thought you knew that."

A merry laugh from a society girl standing directly behind the speaker attracted their attention. "You win, Monty," she said. "Here's the money."

She handed Rollo's brother a certified cheque for thirty-seven thousand dollars.

"You have shown us something new," she said. "This brother of yours is the newest bangle in the showcase. I must have him to tea this afternoon."

"Make it for five, then," said Monty. "I 've got to take him up to Codgers, Feet & Co.'s and dress him first."

"Very well," said the girl. "Only don't be late."

.   .   .   .

"Who was that young lady?" asked Rollo, as he entered Monty's private car, and rode under the river in the tube, and uptown through the subway.

"That is Cora Van Ketcham," said Monty. "She is only twenty-two years old, but she has divorced fourteen husbands already, and has an alimony account of $2,000,000 a year. Some day you will marry her. I 've put you on the waiting list."

"Waiting list?" asked Rollo, perplexed.

"Yes," said Monty. "Cora is an ambitious girl, and is in a fair way to marry all the men in New York. There are forty fiancés ahead of you, so your turn is n't likely to come for a couple of years yet. Meanwhile if you happen to marry anybody else, Rollo, remember that you do not do it permanently. The time is coming when no man will be admitted to New York society who has not at one time or another been married to Cora Van Ketcham."

CHAPTER II

THE train drew up at a station and the guard at the far end of the car called out: "Rarly-Rar-Ree!" in a loud tone of voice.

"What did he say?" asked Rollo.

"He says this is Thirty-eighth Street," explained Monty. "I told him to stop at Codgers, Feet & Co.'s. We must get you a wardrobe. You can't be introduced to Mrs. Chaster in blue jeans and a linen duster."

They mounted the steps and Rollo soon found himself in the clothing emporium of Messrs. Codgers, Feet & Co. A gentlemanly salesman approached and smilingly greeted them.

"Mr. Fytter," said Monty, "you will be good enough to send the contents of this store up to the St. Gotham before two o'clock. We'll take what we want and return the rest."

7

Rollo stood aghast. The St. Gotham was the most expensive hotel in town and the sum total of his ready cash was four dollars, one of which was in Confederate money.

"Really, Monty," he began.

"Don't keep us waiting either, Mr. Fytter," continued Monty. "My brother is paying $8,000 a minute for the apartment and we shall deduct the amount of the rent for every minute you are behind time from your bill.

"The goods will be delivered at one forty-five, Mr. Goitt," replied the smiling Fytter.

"Good," said Monty. "Come along, Rollo; we are due at Colonel Skeeziks's at twelve for luncheon."

CHAPTER III

SO THIS is the son of my old college chum, Major-General Goitt, eh?" asked Colonel Skeeziks ten minutes later. as Rollo, led by Monty, entered Childs's restaurant, which the Colonel had chartered for the day.

"I have often heard my father speak of you, Colonel," said Rollo, modestly.

"Dear old Nicholas!" cried the Colonel, wiping a tear from the end of his nose. "I shall never forget him. In the battle of Blue Forks we sat in opposing trees and peppered each other with bird shot all day long before either of us knew that the retreat had been ordered on both sides."

"He has often told me of that," said Rollo. "And how he lent you $2 to hire a waggon to enable you to catch up with your command."

The Colonel laughed heartily. "Yes," he said. "I remember that loan well. I have that same $2 yet. They were both counter-

9

feit. But now let us eat, my boy. What would you like."

"Anything I can chew," said Rollo, naïvely, for he was very hungry, having had only two doughnuts since he had left Mississippi.

"Bring us a thousand dollars' worth of hard boiled eggs," said the Colonel, turning to the waitress, "and eighty portions of buck-wheat, with nine dollars' worth of the maple juice on the side."

CHAPTER IV

SHALL I wait?" asked the Taxicabman as Rollo and Monty descended at the door of the St. Gotham.

"I don't know," said Monty. "How much do I owe you?"

The Jehu consulted the small clocklike register at the side of the cab.

"Nineteen dollars and sixty cents," he answered.

"Well, wait until I owe you a hundred and thirty-two-thirty," said Monty. "I never pay less than a hundred for a cab."

They entered the onyx and gold corridor of the St. Gotham, where Rollo was delighted to find that Monty, remembering his love for music, had engaged the New York Symphony orchestra to greet him, with a solo by Signor Caruso and a trill of welcome by Mme. Nordica. They then got aboard a special elevator that Monty had had put in for Rollo's use and were shot up forty flights in the air,

11

to the palatial apartment to which reference has already been made. Here they alighted, and Rollo was immediately picked up by a corps of valets and carried into his bedroom, where he was laid gently down upon a Louis Quinze bed, which, had he been a connoisseur, he would have known had cost not less than $38,000 f. o. b. out in Kansas, where all the Louis Quinze antiques are now made.

The apartment was indeed beautiful. From the Riding Academy on the Avenue side to the billiard room and natatorium on the street front the appointments were exquisite and perfect in detail. There was a library of thirty thousand volumes just off the drawing-room, and adjoining the dining-room, where a continuous table d'hôte dinner was served from midnight to midnight, was a small theatre in which, as they entered, a performance of "The Merry Divorcée," the reigning popular success of the season, was going on.

"Gee!" cried Rollo, as he took in all this magnificence at a glance.

"If there is anything you want and don't see, ask for it," laughed Monty, amused at his brother's naïve wonderment.

"Is n't there a church connected with it?" Rollo asked.

"By Jove!" cried Monty, a look of annoyance passing over his face, "I knew I'd forgotten something."

He ran to the telephone. "Is this the office?" he asked, after ringing twice.

"Yes," was the answer.

"Well, send up a cathedral right away, —what's that? Oh!"

Here he paused and turning to Rollo he asked. "Do you want it high or low?"

"Neither," answered Rollo, a streak of economy coming over him. "Just tell 'em to send up a couple of missionaries. They'll do."

CHAPTER V

WHEN the contents of the vans from Codgers, Feet & Co. had been delivered Rollo started to try on the garments that had been sent, when suddenly in the midst of this he felt a poignant pain in his side. He grew very pale, and fell back on the bed.

"I've got a pain to beat the band!" he moaned. "It's those flapjacks."

Monty laughed "You'll do," he said. "It's appendicitis. Could n't be better. We'll have Dr. McCuttem over in a jiffy. He'll have it out in two minutes. It's d —— fashionable Rollo."

"It'll cost like thunder, won't it?" moaned Rollo.

"Oh, no," said Monty. "McCuttem never charges more than $10,000 a cut."

"But how about the tea?" asked Rollo. "I don't want to miss that, Monty."

"You won't," laughed Monty. "That's

one of McCuttem's specialties. It 's all over in half an hour — why, my dear boy, they use operations for appendicitis for german favours in this town."

CHAPTER VI

WHEN Rollo came to after the operation he was delighted with the sensation. He felt as he had not felt since he was a boy when he was known as the champion green apple eater of Mississippi. His side, it is true, was a little numb from the effects of the radium bath to which it had been subjected, but a great weight seemed to have been lifted from it.

"How about my diet, doctor?' he asked as he rose to dress.

"You will have to eat simply for awhile," said the doctor. "Avoid beets, mashed potatoes and milk shakes. Anything else in moderation won't hurt you, and if it does, why, I 'll come around and help you out again. I have a special rate for appendicitis, on a regular commutation basis, grading the cost of secondary, tertiary, and other subsequent operations down until the average cost is not more than $4,000."

"We'll take one of your fifty-trip family tickets, doctor," said Monty. "There's no telling when we'll need you again, but it's well to be on the safe side. Rollo will simply have to eat a couple of Welsh rabbits this afternoon or get out of the game."

The genial surgeon handed Rollo the desired ticket and took his departure. Rollo then took a bath in Chambertin, and was afterward rubbed down by a masseur with a most agreeable solution of crême-de-menthe and champagne. He then dressed in a faultlessly fitting frock coat, a pink waist-coat with gold buttons and a collar made of the purest white ivory. A mauve tie, pinned with a black pearl the size of a hen's egg, completed his façade, and he was ready for the Van Ketcham tea.

"Here's a cheque for $50,000, Rollo," said Monty, as they descended to the street and boarded Monty's $100,000 Limousine, which was waiting at the door. "You may be asked to join in a little rubber of bridge, and if you are careful this ought to last you through the afternoon."

CHAPTER VII

I LIKE New York very much," Rollo was saying to "Dippy" Hollister, a few hours later, as he and she sat on a sofa made of orchids in Mrs. Van Ketcham's conservatory. "But tell me, Dippy, Why do you call this a tea? I 've had six mint juleps, four champagne cocktails, seven bottles of Milwaukee, and a quart of Bronx eye-openers, but nobody has offered me any tea yet."

Miss Hollister's silver laughter rang out through the house and echoed through the drawing-room.

"Only servant girls drink tea, my best beloved," returned the girl. "We have to do something in a republic to show our superiority over the labouring classes. Now order me a couple of rye highballs and let me tell you who these people are."

Rollo summoned the attendant, a gorgeous flunky dressed in red plush, who wheeled in to them a small, compact buffet, containing a completely equipped bar in miniature.

"Better leave the whole thing, Montmorency," said Dippy, as the attendant asked for the orders. "I 've been on the water waggon for two hours and I want to catch up."

CHAPTER VIII

WELL, how did you like the tea, Rollo?" asked Monty, as the patrol wagon drew up at the St. Gotham five hours later and the hotel attendants carried them up to their apartment.

"I did n't have any," said Rollo.

"How did you come out at bridge?" queried the other. "I saw you playing with Susie De Brooch and Tom Collins. They have a system that's hard to beat."

"I won three million dollars in I. O. U.'s," answered Rollo. "But I lit a cigarette with a million dollars' worth and gave the rest to the man who helped me on with this overcoat."

"Splendid!" cried Monty. "I wonder whose overcoat it is. It's sable lined and there's a bunch of Metropolitan bonds in the inside pocket."

"I don't know whom it belongs to," laughed Rollo, "but it 's a peach. I suppose I 'll have to return it to-morrow."

20

"Not on your life," retorted Monty. "Findings is keepings in this town. I did pretty well myself."

Here Monty dove down into his pockets and brought out three dozen solid silver table spoons, a gold card receiver and a lady's vanity bag studded with rubies.

"I'll net sixty thou' on this little deal, myself," he said.

Rollo stood amazed.

"Why, Monty," he cried, "you are n't going to keep them, are you?"

"Sure!" replied Monty. "How do you suppose I do all this, anyhow?"

"Then I'll keep these," said Rollo, taking a soup ladle and a diamond tiara from his coat-tail pocket. "I tried to get away with the piano, but it was too heavy to move."

Monty looked at his brother in admiration, and, slapping him on the back affectionately, he cried, "By Jove, Rollo, I'm proud of you. You'll get ahead all right, all right!"

"Get a head?" retorted Rollo. "Let me tell you, Monty Goitt, I've got a head already! If there's a worse one in New York keep it from me, brother, keep it from me."

And the two brothers curled upon the rug and went to sleep.

CHAPTER IX

WHEN Rollo woke up the next morning he was surprised to find that his valet had already dressed him and that he had had his bath and was ready for the work of the day.

"Well, Monty," he said, as they breakfasted on nine dollars' worth of toast and a case of champagne. "I suppose it is up to me to go looking for a job somewhere this morning."

"What on earth do you want a job for?" demanded Monty. "Are n't you satisfied with the one you 've got?"

"Why, have I got one?" asked Rollo.

"Certainly you have," retorted Monty. "Your job now is to get into society without letting society get into you, and it 's enough to keep any man busy."

"But," protested Rollo, "I have n't got any money, Monty. You know that as well as I do."

"True," said Monty, "but they don't

know it, and what they don't know won't hurt you. Of course, if you want to be a motorman on the subway go ahead and mote, but I tell you right now there is more money to be made on the level. Here's a hundred thousand for you now. It ought to hold you until lunch time, when I shall return to take you to a week-end house party at Bobby Swellings down at Boroughhampton-by-the-Sea. If you need any more, ring up the office, but don't borrow less than twenty thousand. It 'll make 'em suspicious."

"Where are you going?" asked Rollo.

"Shopping," said Monty. "Mrs. Golliver Squidge has asked me to buy a pair of pink silk stockings for her and I know where I can get a pair for eighty cents."

"Mercy!" laughed Rollo. "I did n't suppose Mrs. Golliver Squidge would wear anything costing less than a hundred."

"She would n't if she knew it," smiled Monty. "To save her from mortification I shall see that she never knows."

"You mean to say, Monty, that you will charge Mrs. Golliver Squidge a hundred dollars for an eighty cent pair of stockings?"

"I mean to say," said Monty, "That I shall collect my commission of $99.20. Meanwhile you might put in your morning making out my monthly bills. There's the list."

Monty tossed a slip of paper over to Rollo and calling his motor, departed.

"I wondered where he got it," murmured Rollo.

CHAPTER X

ROLLO glanced over Monty's memorandum and was astonished at the items. One of them read as follows:

Feb. 3—Hiram J. Porkopolis, for one introduction to Hon. Clancey M. Defew.	$1,000
Feb. 4—Escorting Mrs. Porkopolis and daughters to Metropolitan Opera.	2,500
Feb. 5—Escorting Mrs. Porkopolis and daughters to Hammerstein's.	500
Feb. 6—Securing invitation of Mrs. P. and daughters to Mrs. Willie Deuceace's bridge party.	3,000
Feb. 7—For mentioning the elder Miss Porkopolis as an heiress to the Grand Duke of Nitzky	5,000
Feb. 7—Loan to Duke for a suit of clothes in which to call on Miss P.	500
Feb 10—For dining en famille with the Porkopolis family with Duke N.	2,500
Feb. 20—First payment on account of engagement of Duke of Nitzky and Miss Porkopolis	10,000
Total.	$25,000

"Merciful heavens!" cried Rollo. "What a business!"

CHAPTER XI

AT ONE o'clock Monty returned. "I have invited Dippy Hollister and Mrs. Von Boodle to lunch, Rollo," he said. "They'll be here in five minutes. While I am dressing you'd better order. I guess forty cocktails will be enough, and — er — let me see — you might begin with some plum pudding, with stuffed green peppers on the side; follow that with a Welsh rabbit and biscuit tortoni en tasse, some corned beef and cabbage, a couple of saddles of spring lamb, mince pie, an Irish stew, Boston cream cakes and some fish balls. Tell the waiter to put five pitchers of Château Yquem, '68, on the ice, and to have the bathtub filled with Blue Ruinart, Brut. And let me tell you before they come, if Mrs. Von Boodle offers to match you for the lunch don't let any of your foolish notions of Southern chivalry restrain you from letting her pay for it if she loses. It is the truest chivalry to help a woman in dis-

27

tress, and just at present Mrs. Von Boodle's chief cause of worry is her inability to spend her income."

Rollo gave the order, and when the ladies arrived, a few minutes later, everything was in readiness. Mrs. Von Boodle turned out to be a most attractive woman and she and Rollo got on together like a house afire.

"Have you met many people since you arrived?" she asked Rollo.

"Quite a number," said Rollo. "I have found them all very charming. Colonel Skeeziks was good enough to invite me to lunch the day I arrived——"

"Skeeziks? Skeeziks?" said Mrs. Von Boodle. "Seems to me I have heard that name before. Dippy, dear, do I know anybody named Skeeziks — Colonel Skeeziks?"

"Why, yes, Aunt Maria," replied Dippy. "Don't you remember — he was your first husband."

"Oh, well," laughed Mrs. Von Boodle, "that accounts for it. The name sounded familiar. But of course you know, Mr. Goitt, one can't be expected to remember the names of all one's husbands in times like these. Were there any children, Dippy?"

"Two," replied Dippy. "But they never moved in our set, Aunt Maria."

.   .   .   .

"You are a most agreeable young man, Mr. Goitt," said Mrs. Von Boodle, as she paid for the lunch later in the afternoon. "And I hope you will come and see me. You are not engaged to be married, are you?"

"Not yet, Mrs. Von Boodle," Rollo answered with a blush.

"I only asked because I am thinking of divorcing Von Boodle, and there's no telling but that I shall be in the matrimonial market again very soon," said the lady pensively. "You might bear the idea in mind."

Rollo courteously promised to think about it, and the guests took their departure.

"Great Scott!" cried Rollo, when he returned to the apartment. "The old lady has left her gold pocketbook on the mantelpiece."

"That's an old habit of hers," laughed Monty. "How much is there in it?"

"Sixty-eight thousand dollars," said Rollo, counting the money.

"Fine!" ejaculated Monty. "That will pay our tips at the Swelling's house party nicely."

CHAPTER XII

THE meal was over at four o'clock and word came from below stairs that Monty's touring car was waiting.

They boarded the car and started down the avenue. "You 'd better climb into the upper berth, Rollo, and get forty winks. You 'll need 'em before we get back. Nobody ever goes to bed at Swelling's, and when you are new to the game the way you are it 's a tough job keeping awake from Thursday to Tuesday."

Rollo crawled up into the upper berth at the rear of the motor, but he found it impossible to sleep. The excitement of the day had been too much for him and, besides, he did not wish to miss any of the scenery.

"What river is this?" he asked, as the car passed over the East River.

"It 's the East River," said Monty. "It connects Mr. John D. Pocantico's private sound on the north with Colonel Skibo's

31

ocean. Mr. Pocantico is very nice about it and lets the public use it whenever they want to — fact is all these rich men are mighty decent about their property. Colonel Skibo does n't charge a cent when anybody comes along and wants to bathe in his ocean, and you have seen for yourself how Mr. Moneybags permits the children of the poor to play in his Central Park and ride on his street cars."

"And yet they are held up by socialistic writers as being selfish men," said Rollo.

"Yes," said Monty. "They are. It's a great shame, and I don't wonder that a lot of our billionaires are going abroad to live."

As Monty spoke the car turning a sharp curve crashed into a milk wagon and in a moment the scene was bathed in white. "Don't stop," Monty telephoned to the chauffeur. "Chuck out one of those bunches of Transcontinental Bonds and haul in our number."

"We are using Major Skinner's number this afternoon, sir," returned the chauffeur.

"Oh, all right," said Monty. "Let it go then and keep the bonds until we kill a hen."

But the car had to stop nevertheless, for a long chain stretched across the highway ahead made further progress impossible.

"What's the meaning of this, officer?" demanded Monty of the constable, who loomed up alongside of them.

"I wanted to see, sir, if you wished to lodge any complaint against that milkman," said the constable. "His milk is watered, sir."

"You are a vigilant official," said Monty. "Here's three hundred dollars for you. I have n't time to prosecute the milkman, but if he lives you'd better warn him to keep off the public thoroughfares from 6 A. M. to midnight hereafter or we'll have him prosecuted."

"Very good, sir," replied the officer, touchhing his cap respectfully. "I'll tell him, and what's more if he's run into again on my beat I'll club the head off of him."

Barring the killing of four horses, seven dogs and a couple of pigs nothing further occurred to relieve the monotony of the ride down, and at five precisely the car drew up before the Long Island cottage of Bobby Swelling, a beautiful structure, reminding one in its general lines of the Waldorf-Astoria, only larger. Rollo had noticed a couple of buildings on either side of the drive as they entered Swelling Park that looked like a Carnegie Library he had once seen in Pittsburg, and he inquired what they were.

"The one on the left is a hen-house," said Monty. "The other is a servants' hall. Swelling keeps a reserve force of butlers, maids, valets, chefs, scullery maids, chauffeurs, gardeners, pages, and so on, there all the time in case any of those actually employed around the house become incapacitated."

Liveried servants took the car and others carried them into the great house, where Rollo found a large company already assembled playing pinochle. Among others he spied Baby De Bille, a large, ruddy cheeked young maiden, whom he had met at Mrs. Van Ketcham's tea. He had been much impressed by her appetite at that function, and was amused to observe that she was still eating, a broiled squab and a platter of mashed potatoes having been placed on the card table beside her. Miss Tootsie Flyman was also there and was having her hair marcelled while playing.

"We can't afford to lose any time, Mr. Goitt," she remarked, as Rollo greeted her. "I 've got to earn enough money to pay my tips or go home."

"I could n't lend you a couple of hundred, could I," Rollo asked politely.

"I don't think you could n't," she replied roguishly. "Why don't you try?"

Rollo passed on to the next table. Here there were only three players, and his coming was hailed with delight.

"Come on in, the water 's fine," cried Mazie Bunkem. "We 've been wanting a fourth hand ever since Chollie Wiggins slid under the table."

CHAPTER XIII

ROLLO played an indifferent game of pinochle, and as a result when he was carried to his room an hour later to be dressed for dinner he was dimly conscious of having lost between seventy-five and a hundred thousand dollars.

"I 've made a fool of myself, Monty," he groaned, when his brother joined him. "I 've lost nearly a hundred thousand in that dashed game."

"Bully for you," said Monty. "Keep on losing and you 'll be invited everywhere."

"I don't want them to think I can't do anything," retorted Rollo.

"My dear boy, popularity in the metrolopus is not based on what you do, but on the easy grace with which you let yourself be done," said Monty. "Your turn will come at the shoot to-night."

"The shoot?" demanded Rollo.

"Yes," said Monty. "I 've told Swelling

that you are a dead shot, and after supper
he 's going to have a champagne shoot to
give you a chance.''

CHAPTER XIV

ROLLO took the rifle in his hands, and leaning his arm easily upon the dinner table aimed the weapon at the first bottle of Goitt & Shandon on the buffet. The whole company was breathless with interest. Bang went the rifle, and the graceful neck of the champagne bottle shivered into a thousand pieces. Bang went the second shot, and with the same effect upon the second bottle, and so on until he had shot the whole case without a miss.

"Set 'em up again," said Swelling imperturbably.

The butler arranged the contents of another case on the buffet, and Rollo repeated the performance — twenty-four quarts had gone down without a miss.

"I'm game," muttered Swelling. "How many cases have we left, Harlow?" he added addressing the butler.

"Ninety, sir," replied the butler.

"Bring 'em all up," said Swelling. "I'll bet anybody here a million to a nickel he falls down before he finishes the twenty-fifth case."

The bet was promptly accepted on all sides, the women particularly showing great eagerness to get into the game.

"I'll take a hundred thousand dollars' worth of that," said Monty.

Rollo's nerve grew steadier as he realised what a win of that kind would mean to the Goitt family fortunes. A hundred thousand dollars was five million nickels. And if he won Monte would be a winner of five billion dollars or thereabouts on the odds offered by Swelling. Case after case went shivering to pieces before his unerring aim, until only one bottle stood between him and the riches of Golconda. Dippy Hollister, who had ten cents on the result, fainted; and Swelling's face grew livid as he thought of the prospect — not that the sum itself was a large one to a man who owned half of Bensonhurst and carried innumerable small fortunes on margin in most of the bucket shops of New York, but because of the great waste in champagne which Rollo's marksmanship had involved.

"I wish we'd made it beer," he growled to himself.

Again Rollo's rifle came to the aim. His eye flashed down the barrel length, and his hand trembled slightly, but with a short, sharp gasp he pulled the trigger.

BANG!

. . . .

Rollo woke up. "Where am I?" he murmured, and then he looked around him. He was lying in his bed, his comfortable old Mississippi bed, and at his side stood his mother and good old Dr. Bosbyshell, the family physician.

"He will recover," said the doctor, feeling his pulse. "It has been a hard pull, my boy," he added.

"Have I been ill?" gasped Rollo, rubbing his eyes.

"Very," said the doctor. "You have had a bad attack of Yellow Novelitis, I would advise you to give up current literature and confine your reading hereafter to the Little Prudy Books or the Dotty Dimple Series."

"I have been——" queried Rollo.

"Gasphyxiated," returned the doctor, smiling down upon him.

"But Monty!" cried Rollo, unconvinced. "Where is Monty?"

"He is coming home," said his mother. "Poor boy! He telegraphed us last night for the necessary carfare."

And then Rollo understood.

SIX MONTHS

A TALE OF RETRIBUTION, BY HELLINOR
GRYN

CHAPTER I

NOW this is a corollary in a young man's
life, and, like most of the continued
stories of this day and generation, has so little
beginning or ending that the gentle reader
can start in with it at any point, or drop it
at any other, without losing anything in
particular. And you who are old enough to
have read its predecessor through and have
not forgotten what you thought about the
desirability of leaving it around the house
where the children would be likely to get hold
of it may condemn it. But there are others
who never think about such things and to
whom a book's a book for a' that it may contain, who, perhaps, will understand and find
a dollar and a half's worth of interest in the

42

study of what happened to Paul after he had been awakened and had placed his imprint as a publisher upon the novel of a woman who made an illumination of a considerable amount of space.

Paul Greendayne was a publisher, young, fresh, and foolish, when the original episode began. Life was full of uncertainties for him. He was not sure, for instance, that he liked publishing better than anything else in the world, and certainly there was not a fortune in the Little Willie books which had hitherto constituted his list, for the reason that the Sunday-school libraries for which they were designed paid for them for the most part in picture cards and illuminated texts, which in the hard times in which Paul worked were not regarded either as legal tender or as good security at the trust company where Paul kept his poor but honest balance. Nevertheless he had taken it up, and all those who have taken publishing up know how hard it is to let go of it again.

His head ached a good deal this morning and he was disinclined to see any one. His eyes were red with reading, and the perusal of sixty-three pages of "Little Willie on Wall Street" in proofs had given him the temper of to-day, yesterday, and to-morrow all rolled into one. So reticent had he become that he would not even reply to the telephone, which had rung repeatedly during the last hour. Finally, however, he was awakened by a hard, strident whistle from without and a whack upon his door that echoed and re-echoed through his throbbing temples.

Paul's heart beat violently. He felt a pulse, not to say an impulse, in his throat for a few seconds.

"Come in," he said listlessly.

The door was immediately opened and the Japanese office boy entered.

"Well?" said Paul irritably.

The office boy handed him a card. Paul glanced at it and immediately was thrilling all over. He had learned a number of swear words at Harvard, Yale, and Columbia in the various courses in literature he had taken at those universities, as he educated himself by degrees, but none of them seemed to fit into his present mood. Rather was this a moment for expressions of joy, for the card he held in his hand was none other than that of the most distinguished lady authoress of the day. It read —

* * * * * *

Thursday.   London.

"Poor woman!" he murmured softly to himself. "She has brought it to me at last. I wondered if it could possibly get this far along the list."

"Show the lady up — or, rather, in, Niki," he added aloud. "I wish to see if she looks like her pictures."

* * * * * * *

At the first glow of dawn Paul awoke, a strange sensation of elation and apprehension thrilling his veins as his thoughts flew back over the last twenty-four hours, and he realised that he had accepted her manuscript, for there on his desk lay the delicately scented package containing the material for this new venture upon which he had embarked and which was to lift his name out of the dull and sodden purlieus of the Sunday School forever

— it was his to print; her proofs were his to correct; his name and hers would be linked from this time on forever in the imperishable records of the Six Best Sellers of the century. The wildest thrill his life had known then came to Paul; he clasped the manuscript in his arms with a frenzy of mad, passionate joy.

*　*　*　*　*　*　*

CHAPTER XIII

THE reception of the book was so intensely soignée — that is what pleased Paul. He had never thought about such things, or noticed them much in other books that he had published, but this one was a revelation. It might so easily have turned out to be blasé, or even honi soit — there were moments when in the isolation of his own conscience he had even feared that it would prove demi-monde — but now the skies were all sunshine and his fears were at rest. Once while riding on the top of a taxibus with the author, gaining courage from the brisk breeze of that loftier altitude, he had suggested some of these fears to her and had said that possibly some of her readers would think the story immoral.

The lady laughed, and with an insouciance that reached to his very soul above the rush and roar of the street, gazing full into his eyes she had murmured:

"Immoral! It is so quaint a word, my

47

Paul! Each one sees it how they will. For me it is immoral to be false, to be mean, to steal, to cheat, to stoop to low actions and small ends. In this work I have gone in for fine writing and large ends."

"Large ends?" said Paul dreamily.

"Yes, dearest," she replied softly, as she snuggled closer. "Dividends."

The thought of this as ever made Paul thrill, he forgot all other arguments and a quiver ran through him of intense emotion, his eyes swam. The lady, too, leaned back and closed her eyes.

"In my next story, Paul," she said, "I am going to be more frank even than in this one. I am going to say ——"

"Sh!" whispered Paul. "Say it in stars, dear. There's a policeman on the corner."

And she, the glow of the divine fire lighting up her eyes, continued as follows:

         *   *   *   *   *   *   *

         *   *   *   *   *   *   *

         *   *   *   *   *   *   *

and so on.

Paul shivered as she finished. It was all so true, all so beautiful. People did do these things, but until now no one had dared tell of them in print, and it was to him that the great unique opportunity had come, and he owed it all to her!

"O Imperatoffskiwoffski!" he murmured.

It was then that she gave the order for home.

* * * * * * *

CHAPTER XXIII

THE days passed on, March had almost come, and the royalties were due on the first of the month. Several times she had spoken to him of them, and he had gently put her off with sly, humorous allusions to art for art's sake. It was not that he was unwilling or unable to send her a cheque; quite the contrary; but would the check be honoured by the Crackerjack Trust Company? Could it be reorganised in time, and if so would it be paid in full or only in part? It worried Paul intensely. The success had been so obviously great that Vodka had not scrupled to play bridge with members of the Smart Set, and Paul was in a fever of apprehension as to whether or not the Set had proven too smart for her. Her touching appeals to him for advances had filled him with a sodden fear that she was anticipating her income, and that, womanlike, she would not understand when the day of reckoning came why it was

50

that he would be compelled to pay his obligations in deferred debenture reorganisation certificates, payable on January 3, 1947 instead of in Clearing House notes. An overpowering lassitude took hold upon him as he thought of these things, and an intense longing to go back to the publication of Sunday-school books entered into his spirit It was of things like these that Paul was thinking this late February morning. His uncle noticed the daily look of strain, and his friends anxiously inquired if he were dull, and offered all sorts of entertainment to divert him, but Paul resolutely put them off, bravely resolved to meet his cares unaided and alone.

"Maybe she will forget," he said to himself, but it was not to be so. This very morning as he was revolving the difficulties of the situation over in his tired brain Dimity, her Russian maid, came.

"From the Imperatoffskiwoffski, Excellency," he said, handing Paul a note, which he took from the pocket of his sealskin cossak.

"More asterisks?" smiled Paul, wanly.

"I have not read it, Excellency," said the

Russian stolidly. "I don't think, however, that it contains what you fear."

Paul nervously tore open the flap of the envelop and read. Alas, even as Dimity had suggested, it was not stars this time that his divinity had sent him, au contraire, as Paul's faltering eye fell upon the beloved handwriting he saw these burning words:

Dear Paul:

██

█████? R. S. V., Per Dimity;

VODKA.

It was the tensest moment in his life, and when six hours later the janitor of the office building came in to empty the waste basket he found the inert form of Paul Greendayne still lying in a swoon on the floor, Vodka's letter clasped in his hand and the rigid figure of the faithful Dimity standing by the desk, still waiting for the answer he had been instructed to bring back with him.

CHAPTER LVIX

* * * * * * *

* * * * * * *

* * * * * * *

CHAPTER LXXXXIX

THIS warrant," began Paul, his cheeks aflame.

"Is for you," said the officer. "Come!"

They went out together.

CHAPTER MCMVI

PAUL'S face flushed as the judge finished, and in a moment a full realisation of his predicament flashed over him. The announcement of the foreman that the jury had found him guilty without having to read the book through had made little impression upon his mind. For that he had been more or less prepared, but when the judge pronounced sentence he winced. In all his picturings of what lay before him this grim idea had never entered his mind, and even the fact that the sentence acted as a sort of stay of proceedings in the matter of the transfer of the royalties to the author served in no sense as a mitigation of his humiliation. Was it indeed for this that he had striven all these years? Were the ideals which in the first flush of his unawakened youth he had set for himself, and to which until this woman entered into his life he had been true to end in this sordid way? He thought of his uncle, his aunts, the loving care of his cousins, the solicitude of his friends, the happy peacefulness of the hours when as the publisher of the Little Willie books he had been able to look the whole world in the face, and then the cold heartlessness of the court room, with its throngs of curious women, eager photographers and correspondents of the country newspapers sitting there staring at him, snapshotting his every gesture, peering as it were into his very soul, flashed across his vision and a moist little tear trickled down his nose.

"Six months!" he muttered to himself. "And she who wrote the book goes free. I who merely printed the thing must suffer, but she ——"

The words that he had learned at Harvard, and Yale, and Columbia surged madly up in his throat, but died there as a soft touch at his elbow caused him to turn. It was such a relief to find that it was not the sheriff, but Dimity, her maid, that all resentment vanished from his heart.

"Well?" said he hoarsely.

"From her," replied Dimity, impassively thrusting a letter into his hand.

The court room was silent as the tomb,
and every eye was upon the unfortunate man.
But Paul saw only the dear handwriting on
the envelope, how dear his present plight
could testify to the world. Oh, if that hand
had never learned to write! He seized it
passionately, and with a nervous movement
of the right forefinger tore it open.

DEAREST: **** ***** * *** **! ***** ****?
** **** **** *** *** ******!! **** *** ***
**** *****   VODKA.

That was all.

"Thank God!" cried Paul. "If she had
used words there instead of asterisks I'd
have got ten years."

Then, turning to the Sheriff, he drew himself proudly erect.

"I am ready," said he. "What time does
the first boat to the Island leave?"

EDITOR'S NOTE.—Referring to the omis-
sions in the above extracts from Miss Gryn's
novel the Editor wishes to announce that the
paragraphs presented contain all the news
that's fit to print.

THE LOST SECRET

By E. FILLIPS DOPENHEIM

CHAPTER I

ROOM NO. 4114423

PLACING my suit case on the broad mahogany counter I registered, and flashed one of my most winning smiles upon the diamond-studded room clerk.

"I should like a single room on the twenty-third floor, southwest, about the fifth lateral corridor, and a bath," I said.

He shook his head at once. "I am sorry, Mr. Bravado," he said, "but all the rooms on that floor have been engaged, and as for the bath, they are all taken. If you can wait until Saturday night, which is our regular bath night, I think I can accommodate you. If a finger bowl will help you out ——"

I was about to close with his offer, for,

after all, I had bathed three days before and did not really need to repeat the ordeal quite so soon again, when the junior clerk took his place.

"Don't mind what he says, Mr. Bravado," said the junior. "He does n't come into this story again, and he 's jealous. He knows darned well that if he does n't give you what you have asked for, the tale will have to stop right here on the first page. You can have any room in the house you want, and if you find any baths lying around loose, hot, cold, tepid, or merely lukewarm, take 'em. You 'll find a towel on every floor."

It was thus that I got the room I wanted, No. 4114423, where my friend the novelist had bade me go to await developments. In the light of what occurred afterward I have often wondered what happened to the junior clerk, who gave me the room. Whatever it was I hope he got it good and hard.

CHAPTER II

A MIDNIGHT VISIT

HAVING finished my cigarette, I turned over to go to sleep. So far nothing had happened, and I began to wonder if my old friend Dopenheim had sent me to the wrong hotel. However, this was no business of mine. He was paying my expenses and any loss of time was his and not mine to pay for. It was just midnight — I knew that from the swish of carpet sweepers out in the corridor — when a series of muffled curses from the adjoining room fell upon my ear. Feverishly I reached for the electric light button and soon found it, but one might as well have pushed the nose of a messenger boy as that button, for to my horror I now realized that the wires had been cut? Dopenheim was at work. The row in the adjoining room grew in intensity.

"You must!" cried a strident voice, angrily.

"I shan't!" was the firm response.

"By the Lord Harry ——" cried the first speaker.

"D—nation!" This in muffled tones from a third.

"It is useless!" moaned the second. "I do not know it!"

"Take that!" roared the other two simultaneously.

There was a sound as of some one being hit on the head with a water-pitcher, and then all was silent.

"Is he dead?" came a soft feminine voice.

"As a doornail."

I sat up in bed, with a tense ear placed against the wall, and even as I did so the door communicating with my room and the scene of what I feared was murder was burst open, a heavy object was hurled upon the bed alongside of me, and my visitors, whoever they were, tiptoed lightly out of the room. In the light from the corridor streaming in through the transom I could make out little beyond the fact that there were three of them, but I could hear the delicate swish of a skirt and a slight odour of talcum powder permeated the air.

I knew at once that my future wife was mixed up in this mysterious affair.

CHAPTER III

A GRUESOME DISCOVERY

IT WAS dawn when I awoke. At first the incidents of the night before came into my mind as merely the details of a horrible dream, but the dread reality of the affair was soon borne in upon me. Turning over to take my beauty sleep I was amazed to find that I was not alone in the room. Lying limply across the foot of my bed was an utter stranger, or rather all that remained of one.

"Great heavens!" I muttered. "They have left the poor devil on my hands!"

I sprang out of bed and grasped his nerveless hand. It was cold and rigid and his pulse no longer even fitfully throbbed. The horror of my position at once revealed itself to me. A murder had been committed and here was I caught with the goods! Fortunately my stepbrother, Lord Gregory Bravado, owned a share of stock in the hotel corporation, and doubtless the manager would help me out of my predicament. Rushing to the telephone I rang up the office.

"Give me the manager at once," I 'phoned.

"The manager can only be seen between twelve and one on alternate Thursdays in February," was the curt response. And it was now the 1st of March!

Left thus to my own resources I saw immediately that there was only one thing to be done. To leave the hotel with haste was my first impulse, but it would never do to leave the circumstantial evidence of the crime behind me. It and I must go together, but how to get it out without attracting the attention of the police was a serious question. The victim was a full sized man, and to get him into my suit case was impossible. There was no place in which to conceal him.

There was a knock on my door, followed again by the soft swishing of skirts, as of some one hurrying down the corridor. I opened the door and looked out, but the corridor was empty, but standing in front of the door was a large wardrobe trunk, covered with labels, showing not only that its owner was a much travelled person but was also an American.

"My wife to be is a thoughtful young person," I thought, as I hauled the trunk into the room. "This trunk appears to be just the right size for you," I added, addressing the victim of the tragedy, and indeed my eye did not deceive me, for he fitted it perfectly. I was not long in packing him into it, and then I dressed for breakfast.

"A note for you, sir," said the head waiter, as I entered the dining-room.

"From her!" I murmured, tearing it open feverishly.

But it was not so — merely an engraved invitation from the management requesting me to leave the hotel at once and not to take my room key with me. No word of explanation of the reasons; just a plain, curt intimation that my room was preferable to my company. At first I was inclined to be resentful, and then the thought of the contents of that trunk flashed across my mind, and I realised that I was in no position to be quarrelsome.

"All right," I said, biting my lip to conceal

my vexation. "Tell the porter to bring my luggage down. I leave on the nine-eighteen from Charing Cross."

I finished my breakfast sullenly, paid my cheque and left the dining room. As I passed through the office I noticed the proprietor standing by the elevator, conversing with one of the most beautiful women I have ever seen — tall, dignified, and majestic. In her arms she held a Boston terrier, who showed his teeth like a dentifrice advertisement as his eye lighted upon me. As I appeared the two drew apart, and the lady, gathering her skirts tightly about her so that they should not swish, walked by me, her nose held haughtily high in the air.

But I was not to be deceived. There being no swish of her skirts I could not identify her by that, but in her train, as I turned to gaze after her, there was that which told me who she was — my future wife. The delicate odour of the talcum powder betrayed her.

An hour later I was on my way to Wogley-Wimpleton, the ancestral home of the Bravados, and in the compartment beside me I carried the wardrobe trunk with its grizzly contents.

CHAPTER IV

"WORTLEY WIGGS THE SPY"

SHALL I unpack the trunk, sir?" asked my valet the next morning.

"No, Wobbleton," said I. "It contains nothing of value. You may leave it in the hall for the present."

Wobbleton had been a trusted employee in my family for years, but I was not ready yet to take even him into my confidence.

"I only arsked, sir," said he, "because the gentleman has requested me to bring him a brandy and soda, sir, and a boiled hegg."

"What gentleman?" I roared in astonishment.

"The gentleman as came down in the trunk sir," returned Wobbleton impassively.

"Is he alive?" I cried, springing to my feet.

"As to that I car n't si, sir," returned the valet. "I ar n't never seen him, sir; but

67

'e 'ollered 'is horders through the key 'ole, sir, and I fawncy 'e ain't as dead as some, sir."

A moment later I had the trunk open, and as the cover was raised there rose with it the form of the man I had supposed to have been murdered!

"Heavens!" I cried, "what is the meaning of this?"

"They hit me on the head with a bottle of knock-out drops," he replied. "It takes more than that to kill Wortley Wiggs the Spy."

"You are ——" I began, shrinking back in amazement.

"I am!" said he. "Boil that egg two minutes, Wobbleton," he added, addressing my valet, "I'll take the brandy and soda raw."

CHAPTER V

AN UNWELCOME VISITOR

THE front door bell rang. Wortley Wiggs paled.

"It is Stanley," he muttered. "Curse him! Tell him I am not at home!"

He pulled the cover of the trunk down over himself again and all was still.

"A Mr. Stanley to see you, sir," said Wobbleton, returning from the door.

"I am not in," said I, curtly.

"Oh, yes you are!" observed a short, pudgy looking man who had followed Wobbleton in. "But my advice to you is to get out as quickly as you can. This is no affair of yours, sir, and I hate to see a nice young man like yourself butting into a fracas with which he has no proper concern."

"Who are you?" I demanded.

"I am the villain in this story," he answered insolently. "And I tell you right now that old Bill Stanley is always on his job."

"Suppose I were to kick you out the back door?" I asked, sizing the man up.

"I should immediately run around to the front door and call again, Mr. Bravado," he said. "It's no use, you see. I killed Wortley Wiggs the other night and I intend to have his remains to show to the Amalgamated Brotherhood of Dopenheim Villains in proof that I have fulfilled my mission."

Here was hope. Stanley evidently was not aware that Wortley Wiggs had come to life again. I must temporise.

"You have taken me unawares, Mr. Stanley," said I. "If you will call again to-morrow, I'll see what can be done. You of course cannot expect me to give you anything you may choose to demand without presenting your credentials. As for me, I will hand over the property in question to the village coroner, and if you can prove your ownership I have no doubt he will give you all that is coming to you. Good morning sir. Wobbleton, kick Mr. Stanley out of the window and then close the shutters."

. . . .

That night Wortley Wiggs and I set sail for America, and as the ocean greyhound drew out into the waters of the Mersey I breathed a sigh of relief. We had left our pursuers safely behind!

But alas for our fancied security! As I walked the deck that night a vicious little Boston terrier, whose teeth seemed strangely familiar to me, sprang upon me and fastened his jaws firmly in the lush folds of my trousers.

"Down, Charge," came a soft feminine voice from the depths of a steamer chair, invisible in the blackness of the night; and even as that voice fell upon my ears, in spite of the gale that was blowing, the delicate odour of talcum powder again maddened my nostrils, and with a terrible sinking of my heart I realised that I still had my future wife to reckon with, and worst of all I did not even know her name!

CHAPTER VI

ON BOARD THE "DIGESTIC"

FOR three days hostilities were suspended. All the dramatic personæ of my friend Dopenheim were prostrated by *mal de mer* excepting myself, and even I was not feeling very fit, suffering greatly from nervous headache and frequent attacks of nausea. On the fourth day out Wortley Wiggs, booked for the passage as my valet, turned wearily in his upper berth and gazed mournfully at me.

"It 's no use, Bravado," he said. "I can't go on any longer. The damned motion of this old tub is such that I have resolved to throw up everything. Send Dopenheim a wireless and tell him that we 've all struck."

"Oh, don't give up the ship, old man," I said, trying to cheer him.

"I 've given up everything else," he said, moodily. "What 's the good of going on?

72

To begin with, this story is all about a secret. But what the devil is the secret? I don't know what it is. Stanley does n't know what it is. Miss Van Slathers does n't know what it is. The bull pup does n't know what it is, and I 'll be eternally gollyswazzled if I think old Dope knows what it is."

"That 's very likely true," I said reflectively. "But even so, my friend, my future wife is involved in this thing, and I have got to see my way clear before I desert. I am a Bravado, and our motto is 'Semper Bravado Sic Non Skiddoo.' "

"Then," returned Wortley Wiggs desperately, "nothing is left me but this!"

He sprang from his berth, and before I could stop him he had rushed out of the stateroom and with a mad yell hurled a dynamite bomb into the engine room!

There was a terrific explosion; the vessel shivered and shook; the huge iron sides of the devoted ship bulged out and mountains of water rushed in where once there had been staunch steel walls.

CHAPTER VII

NEMESIS

SAVE me!"
"It was her voice, at the far end of the promenade deck, and as it came to me again that delicious scent of the talcum once more greeted my nostrils. It spurred me into action, and rushing past the smoking room to where she had been sitting, I found her, and that accursed villain Stanley was standing at her side.

"Out of the way, you brute!" I cried, hurling him over the rail into the raging sea. "If it had n't been for you we 'd have been safe on shore to-day."

She gasped. "You don't know what you have done!" she moaned. "That man is not Mr. Stanley, it is Monsieur the Duc de Chanson ——"

"Let the Duc swim," I retorted savagely, putting on my rubbers, for the sea was wet.

"He is the true King of France," she went

74

on. "Papa was going to finance a revolution for him that was to make us all dukes and duchesses!"

"Tell your father to save his money for a better cause," I shouted, as the mad waters began to gurgle at our feet. "I can invest it for him in a nice little farm property I know of at Wogley-Wimpleton. There's quite a leak in my ancestral roof."

"Ah!" she cried passionately. "It is my money you are after, is it?" She drew away from me.

"No, sweetheart," I answered, taking her hand in mine, and realising of how little value money was to either of us at that moment. "I love you for yourself alone. Come!"

"My beloved!" she faltered, placing her damp little cheek upon my shoulder with a deep sigh of content.

The deck of the great vessel gave a lurch and we went down together.

The Dopenheim Novel was lost in the raging depths of the Atlantic!

A PRAGMATIC ENIGMA

BEING A CHAPTER FROM "THE FAILURES OF SHERLOCK HOLMES," BY A. CONAN WATSON, M. D.

IT WAS a drizzly morning in November. Holmes and I had just arrived at Boston, where he was to lecture that night on "The Relation of Cigar Stumps to Crime" before the Browning Club of the Back Bay, and he was playfully indulging in some deductive pranks at my expense.

"You are a doctor by profession, with a slight leaning toward literature," he observed, rolling up a small pill for his opium pipe and placing it in the bowl. "You have just come on a long journey over the ocean and have finished up with a five hour trip on the New York, New Haven and Hartford Railroad. You were brushed off by a coloured porter and rewarded him with a sixpence taken from your right hand vest pocket before leaving the train. You came from the station in a cab, accompanied by a very handsome and famous Englishman; ate a lunch of baked beans and brown bread, opening with a Martini cocktail, and you are now wondering which one of the Boston newspapers pays the highest rates for press notices."

"Marvellous! Marvellous!" I cried. "How on earth do you know all this?" — for it was every bit of it true.

"It is the thing that we see the most clearly that we perceive the more quickly, my dear Watson," he replied, with a deprecatory gesture. "To begin with, I know you are a doctor because I have been a patient of yours for many years. That you have an inclination toward literature is shown by the fact that the nails on the fingers of your right hand are broken off short by persistent banging on the keys of a typewriting machine, which you carry with you wherever you go and with which you keep me awake every night, whether we are at a hotel or travelling on a sleeping car. If this were not enough to prove it I can clinch the fact by calling your attention to the other fact that I pay you a salary to write me up and can produce signed receipts on demand."

"Wonderful," said I; "but how did you know I had come on a long journey, partly by sea and partly by rail on a road which you specify?"

"It is simplicity itself," returned Holmes wearily. "I crossed on the steamer with you. As for the railroad, the soot that still remains in your ears and mottles your nose is identical with that which decorates my own features. Having got mine on the New Haven and Hartford, I deduce that you got yours there also. As for the coloured porter, they have only coloured porters on those trains for the reason that they show the effects of dust and soot less than white porters would. That he brushed you off is shown by the streaks of gray on your white vest where his brush left its marks. Over your vest pocket is the mark of your thumb, showing that you reached into that pocket for the only bit of coin you possessed, a sixpence."

"You are a marvel," I murmured. "And the cab?"

"The top of your beaver hat is ruffed the

wrong way where you rubbed it on the curtain roller as you entered the cab." said Holmes. "The handsome and famous Englishman who accompanied you is obvious. I am he, and am therefore sure of my deduction."

"But the lunch, Holmes, the lunch, with the beans and the cocktail," I cried.

"Can you deny them?" he demanded.

"No, I cannot," I replied, for to tell the truth his statement of the items was absolutely correct. "But how, how, my dear fellow, can you have deduced a bean? That's what stumps me."

Holmes laughed.

"You are not observant, my dear Watson," he said. "How could I help knowing when I paid the bill?"

In proof he tossed me the luncheon cheque, and there it was, itemised in full.

"Aha!" I cried, "but how do you know that I am wondering which one of the Boston papers pays the best rates for press notices?"

"That," said he, "is merely a guess, my dear Watson. I don't know it, but I do know you."

And this was the man they had said was losing his powers!

At this moment there came a timid knock on our door.

"A would-be client," said Holmes. "The timidity of his knock shows that he is not a reporter. If it were the chambermaid, knowing that there were gentlemen in the room she would have entered without knocking. He is a distinguished man, also, who does not wish it known that he is calling, for if it were otherwise he would have been announced on the telephone from the office — a Harvard professor, I take it, for no other kind of living creature in Boston would admit that there was anything he did not know, and therefore no other kind of a Bostonian would seek my assistance. Come in."

The door opened and a rather distinguished looking old gentleman carrying a suit case and an umbrella entered.

"Good morning, professor," said Holmes, rising and holding out his right hand in genial fashion and taking his visitor's hat with his left. "How are things out at Cambridge this morning?"

"Marvellous! Marvellous!" ejaculated the visitor, infringing somewhat on my copyright, in fact taking the very words out of my mouth. "How did you know I was a professor at Harvard?"

"By the matriculation mark on your right forefinger," said Holmes, "and also by the way in which you carry your umbrella, which you hold not as if it were a walking stick, but as if it were a pointer with which you were about to demonstrate something on a chart, for the benefit of a number of football players taking a four years' course in Life, at an institution of learning. Moreover, your address is pasted in your hat, which I have just taken from you and placed on the table. You have come to me for assistance, and your entanglement is purely intellectual, not spiritual. You have not committed a crime nor are you the victim of one — I can tell that by looking at your eyes, which are red, not with weeping, but from reading and writing. The tear ducts have not been used for years. Hence I judge that you have written a book, and after having published it, you suddenly discover that you don't know what it means yourself, and inasmuch as the critics over the country are beginning to ask you to explain it you are in a most embarrassing position. You must either keep silent, which is a great trial to a college professor, especially a Harvard professor, or you must acknowledge that you cannot explain — a dreadful alternative. In that bag you have the original manuscript of the book, which you desire to leave with me, in order that I may read it and if possible detect the thought, tell you what it is, and thus rid you of your dilemma."

"You are a wonderful man, Mr. Holmes," began our visitor, "but if you will let me ——"

"One moment, please," said Holmes, eying the other closely. "Let us deduce next, if possible, just who you are. First let us admit that you are the author of a recently published book which nobody understands. Now, what is that book? It cannot be 'Six Months' by Helinor Quinn, for you are a gentleman, and no gentleman would have written a book of that character. Moreover, everybody knows just what that book means. The book we are after is one that cannot be understood without the assistance of a master like myself. Who writes such books? You may safely assert that the only books that nobody can understand these days are written by one James — Henry James. So far so good. But you are not Henry James, for Henry James is now in London translating his earlier works into Esperanto. Now, a man cannot be in London and in Boston at one and the same time. What is the inevitable conclusion? You must be some other James!"

The hand of our visitor trembled slightly as the marvellous deductive powers of Holmes unfolded themselves.

"Murmarvellulous!" he stammered.

"Now, what James can you be if you are not Henry?" said Holmes, "and what book have you written that defies the interpretation of the ordinary mind hitherto fed on the classic output of Hall Caine, Laura Jean Libbey and Gertrude Atherton? A search of the Six Best Sellers fails to reveal the answer Therefore the work is not fiction. I do not recall seeing it on the table of the reading room downstairs, and it is not likely, then, to be statistical. It was not handed me to read in the barber shop while having my hair cut and my chin manicured, from which I deduce that it is not humour. It is likely, then, that it is a volume either of history or philosophy. Now, in this country to-day people are too busy taking care of the large consignments of history in the making that come every day from Washington in the form of newspaper dispatches to devote any time to the history that was made in the past, and it is therefore not at all probable that you would go to the expense of publishing a book dealing with it. What, then, must we conclude? To me it is clear that you are therefore a man named James who has written a book on philosophy which nobody understands but yourself, and even you——"

"Say no more!" cried our visitor, rising and walking excitedly about the room. "You are the most amazingly astonishing bit of stupefying dumfounderment that I have ever stared at!"

"In short," continued Holmes, pointing his finger sternly at the other, "you are the man who wrote that airy trifle called 'Pragmatism!' "

There was silence for a moment, and then the Professor spoke up.

"I do not understand it at all," he said.

"What, pragmatism?" asked Holmes with a chuckle.

"No, you," returned the Professor coldly.

"Oh, it's all simple enough," said Holmes. "You were pointed out to me in the dining-room at luncheon time by the head waiter, and, besides, your name is painted on the end of your suit case. How could your identity escape me?"

"Nevertheless," said the Professor, with a puzzled look on his face, "granted that you could deduce all these things as to my name, vocation, and so on, what could have given you the idea that I do not myself know what I meant when I wrote my book? Can you explain that?"

"That, my dear Professor, is the simplest of my deductions," said Holmes. "I have read the book."

Here the great man threw himself back in his chair and closed his eyes, and I, realising that I was about to be a witness of a memorable adventure, retired to an escritoire over by the window to take down in shorthand what Holmes said. The Professor, on the other hand, was walking nervously up and down the room.

"Well," said he, "even if you have read it, what does that prove?"

"I will tell you," said Holmes, going into one of his trances. "I read it first as a man should read a book, from first page to last, and when I got through I could not for the life of me detect your drift. A second reading in the same way left me more mystified than before, so I decided to read it backward. Inverted it was somewhat clarified but not convincing, so I tried to read it standing on my head, skipping alternate pages as I read forward, and taking in the omitted ones on the return trip. The only result of this was a nervous headache. But my blood was up. I vowed to detect your thought if it cost me my life. Removing the covers of the book, I cut the pages up into slips, each the size of a playing card, pasted these upon four packs of cards, shuffled them three times, cut them twice, dealt them to three imaginary friends seated about a circular table and played an equally imaginary game of muggins with them, at the end of which I placed the four packs one on top of the other, shuffled them twice again, and sat down to read the pages in the resulting sequence. Still the meaning of pragmatism eluded me."

There was a prolonged pause, interrupted only by the heavy breathing of the Professor.

"Go on," he said hoarsely.

"Well," said Holmes, "as a last resort I sent the book to a young friend of mine who runs a printing shop and had him set the whole thing in type, which I afterward pied, sweeping up the remains in a barrel and then drawing them out letter by letter, arranging them in the order in which they came. Of the result I drew galley proofs, and would you believe it, Professor, when I again proceeded to read your words the thing meant even less than it did before. From all of which I deduce that you did not know what pragmatism was, for if you had known the chances are you would have told us. Eh?"

I awaited the answer, looking out of the window, for the demolition of another man is not a pleasant thing to witness, even though it involves a triumph for one of our most respected and profitable heroes. Strange to say the answer did not come, and on turning to see the reason why I observed to my astonishment that Holmes and I were alone, and, what was worse, our visitor had vanished with both our suit cases and my overcoat as well.

Holmes, opening his eyes at the same moment, took in the situation as soon as I did and sprang immediately to the 'phone, but even as he took down the receiver the instrument rang of itself.

"Hello," said he, impatiently.

"Is this Mr. Holmes?" came a voice.

"Yes," replied the detective, irritably. "Hurry up and get off the wire. I want to call the police. I 've been robbed."

"Yes, I know," said the voice. "I 'm the thief, Mr. Holmes. I wanted to tell you not to worry. Your stuff will be returned to you as soon as we have had it photographed for the illustration of an article in to-night's Boston Gazoozle. It will be on the newsstands in about an hour. Better read it; it 's a corker; and much obliged to you for the material."

"Well, I 'll be blanked!" cried Holmes,

the 'phone receiver dropping from his nerveless fingers. "I fear, my dear Watson, that, in the language of this abominable country, I 've been stung!"

.   .   .   .

Two hours later the streets of Boston were ringing with the cries of newsboys selling copies of the five o'clock extra of the Evening Gazoozle, containing a most offensive article, with the following headlines:

DO DETECTIVES DETECT?

A GAZOOZLE REPORTER DISGUISED AS A HARVARD PROFESSOR

Calls on Sherlock Holmes, Esq.
And Gets Away with Two Suit Cases
Full of the Great Detective's
Personal Effects, While
Dr. Watson's Hero
Tells What He Does Not Know About
PRAGMATISM

THE STEP-DAUGHTER OF PETERSON JAY

By GEORGE JARR McCLUTCHEM

CHAPTER I

PETERSON JAY, DETECTIVE

HE WAS imposing even in his expensiveness. To Tankletown there was no denying the fact that he was a costly official, his salary as Town Marshal adding not less than nine dollars a year to the tax list. For twenty-eight years had Peterson Jay served the town in this capacity, indicating his term of service by the purchase of a new nickel star upon each successive anniversary of his election, wherewith he adorned his person, so that now as he leaned against the village pump, chewing a dandelion stalk and wearing all his badges, he resembled a prosperous

90

Christmas tree far more than a Police Commissioner. His had been a proud record.

"He's saved this here taown thaousands of dollars," said Alf Boozeling, the official drunkard of Tankletown.

"Don't see haow," retorted Ed Stiggins, the Prune King, "He ain't never arrested nobody."

"That's jest it," said Alf. "We ain't hed no jail expenses to pay, hev we?"

It was doubtless of this record that Peterson Jay was thinking, as in his starry splendour he leaned against the pump, in blissful unconsciousness that even then he was standing on the brink of complications of so epoch-making a kind that they would be remembered, if not forever, at least through 346 pages of a Six Best Seller that would rival the works of Dickens or Libbey, in the hearts of girls' boarding schools, wherever located on this broad American continent.

"Whoa!" cried a hoarse voice directly in front of him.

"I dee-duce from thet there voice thet there's a horse somewhere in this here neighbourhood," thought Peterson Jay, and deserting the spiritual Paterson in which his mind had been wandering he observed, with no little pride in his own discernment, that his deductions were correct. A horse indeed had first thrust its nose into his, and had then begun to nibble at the edges of his straw hat, doubtless taking it for a sprig of that local laurel with which the farmers of Tankletown had crowned their honoured Chief of Police.

"Hold my horse a minute, Rube," said the driver of the beast, a handsome young man, set up like the fiancé of a Gibson Girl, tossing the reins at Peterson. "I want to go into yon Prunery and buy a match."

"Hi, thar," retorted Peterson, with dignity. "What do you take me for? A hitchin' post?"

"No," laughed the other, as he entered Stiggins's grocery. "You look to me more like a stranded all-star comic opera troupe waiting for some kind angel to come along and build them a railroad so that they can walk home on the ties. That 's why I offered you a job."

"Thet feller 's criminal," muttered Peterson Jay. "I 'll go up to the haouse and git my gun and foller him, 'y Gorry!"

But when he returned the handsome young desperado had gone on, and what is more the news had come in over seven telephones at once that some one, taking advantage of the blackness of the night before, had rifled Mose Lamson's drying yard of his boiled shirt.

"'T was him!" cried Peterson. "I noticed the varmint had on a biled shirt, an' I thought at the time it looked derned familiar."

And, backed by the village apothecary, the grocer's boy and Bill Mink, the postmaster, Peterson Jay started in pursuit.

CHAPTER II

THE DAUGHTER ON THE STEP

TEN hours later Peterson Jay, having been apprised by his intended victim, whom he had run to earth at the Mayor's office in the adjoining town, getting married, that not only was the shirt he wore his own, as was easily proven by the initials of his best man embroidered on the tab, but that moreover Mose Lamson's missing garment had been found in his next door neighbour's well, whither it had been blown by a pranksome breeze, returned to Tankletown defeated, but not discouraged.

"I 'll bet he stole the cuff buttons, anyhow," he muttered. "I 'll land him yit!"

The night was stormy and Peterson and his wife, after a light supper, retired at about half-past six and were soon wrapped in slumber. Mrs. Peterson, however, was restless, and as the clock struck eight she rose and went below to boil Peterson's egg for his breakfast the next morning. The egg had not been in the kettle more than twenty minutes when a strange sound upon the front porch startled her.

"Peterson," she called upstairs in a loud whisper, "I think they's a burglar on the front piazzy."

"Tell him to go raound to th' jail and make himself to hum for the night," replied the sleepy detective. "This ain't no kind of a night to ask a detective to go out."

"Whar's the key?" demanded Mrs. Peterson.

"Hangin' on the nail on the back of the pianny," said Peterson.

Mrs. Peterson secured the key to the village lock-up, and opening the parlour window, called out into the blackness of the night:

"Here you, Mr. Burglar, here's the key to the jail. Peterson says for you to go lock yourself up. He'll be raound in the mornin,'" she said, her teeth chattering with the cold, although they were made of porcelain.

But there was no answer. Only the muffled wail of a baby from somewhere in the dark.

"Sakes alive!" cried Mrs. Peterson. "It's a baby! Peterson!" she roared, calling up to him again. "He says he ain't a burglar, but a baby."

"Wait till I get my gun, an' I'll be daown," said Peterson.

A few minutes later the town marshal, discreetly sheltered behind the ample proportions of his wife, crept cautiously out upon the piazza, on which the snow now lay ten inches deep.

"Gol-derned good thing I went to bed with my fishin' boots on," he said.

And then his eye fell upon a basket on the lower step of the porch, and in that basket, swathed in old newspapers, lay a bright faced, sunny eyed little lady — just the kind to grow up into a lovely cover in five colours for a popular novel.

"Gosh-all-Hemlocks!" ejaculated Peterson. "Another mystery — I'll have to git my sal'ry raised next taown meetin'."

"She shall be our daughter," said the good wife, her eyes filled with fast melting snow.

"Huh!" said Peterson. "You ain't got

no deductive faculties — women never has. We found her on the step, did n't we?"

"Wa-al, s'posin' we did, Peterson?" said the old lady.

"Wa-al, that makes her our stepdaughter," said Peterson. "But, Gosh-tamitey, I don't know 's we kin afford another, Eva. Times is powerful bad."

"That will be all right," returned Mrs. Peterson, who had been investigating the basket. "Here 's a postal card in the little gal's vanity bag sayin' that her folks 'll send send us two dollars a year for her keep for the next thutty years."

"Two dollars a year!" roared Peterson, his face brightening. "By Heck, Eva, that 's sixty dollars all told! I kin afford to buy one o' them near-gold badges like them taown deetectives wears on that. Bring the child in, an' give her a glass o' nice warm watter. Hang the expense!"

Thus did Rosalie Spink find her foster-parents.

"Somebody must ha' left her there," mused Peterson, shaking his finger at the bedpost, "and I don't propose to go to sleep until I find out who."

Whereupon he went back to bed, and five minutes later was slumbering profoundly and dreaming that the sixty dollars had already been paid.

CHAPTER III

KIDNAPPED

IT DID not take long for the thirty years to pass by — ten pages at most, and one of these with an illustration on it. Year by year the promised two dollars arrived regularly and persistently — sometimes as much as two dollars and sixty cents; and numerous packages also came by express to Rosalie, containing gowns by the best modistes between Paris and New York, so that Rosalie was always the most stylishy dressed person in all Tankletown. But the mystery of her parentage, in spite of Peterson's unremitting endeavours to unravel it, remained as deep as ever. Alf Boozeling, being a man and unmarried, soon acquitted himself of all suspicion of being the child's mother, when Peterson Jay indirectly accused him of that particular crime; Ed Stiggins had more children than he knew what to do with, anyhow and as for the rest of the town, everybody else was too stingy even to offer to pay sixty dollars for her keep, much less pay it.

" 'Pears to me," said Peterson Jay as he polished up his nickel plated stars, " 'pears to me 's if her parients must ha' been outsiders."

As Rosalie grew to glorious young womanhood some thirty or forty Mary Wilkins characters living in Tankletown proposed marriage to her. Rosalie was easily the belle of the village, for as 'Rast Bunker said, "she 's a light feeder and they ain't no mother-in-law throwed in." But to every one of these ardent swains Rosalie's answer was the same. It could not be. She liked them and their honest, homespun ways, but in one of the packages from her mysterious benefactors — the one containing her subscription to a complete college education in one of the magazine correspondence schools, from which she had learned in ten easy lessons to speak French like a native — of Boston — and had acquired her intense love for Emerson, and had got so that she could tell Wagner from DeKoven on Daddy Jay's gramophone —

in this package, I say, had come one of her creator's own beautiful novels, and secretly, without even knowing it herself, Rosalie was saving her own avowals of imperishable love for one who should come later; one who would wear a fascinating green mackintosh and a muffler of silk about his neck; to whom a boiled shirt was a necessity of everyday life, not an occasional social diversion, as in the case of Hank Willerby; who should wear also a gray felt hat with the front rim pulled down and the back rim turned up, and tan gloves and patent leather pumps, and carry a cane, and prove himself the hero he was intended to be. Him she would wait for if it took two hundred and fifty pages to bring him on the scene. And then in the midst of these pastoral scenes and maidenly reflections came the awful tragedy for which everybody had been waiting all these interminable years. Rosalie was kidnapped on the eve of her thirtieth birthday.

Peterson Jay had just returned from a vain effort to locate a ghost that had been stealing chickens at the haunted house up near Boggs' Corners.

"Hi, Dad!" cried his son Roscoe, rushing out of the house to greet him, "Rosalie's been stole!"

The old man's face went ashen gray and he staggered.

"What?" he cried.

"Rosalie's been stole!" repeated the lad.

Peterson sat down to think on the horse trough. His deductive faculties were summoned into instant operation, and his sympathetic but admiring neighbours awaited the results of his cogitations with a breathless interest. At last he apoke.

" 'Y gorry!" he said, bringing his hand down with a terrific whack on his knee. "Ef she's been stole ——"

"Yes?" cried Alf Boozeling, who could scarce contain himself with excitement.

"Then," said the old man deliberately and with an air of finality, "then somebody must ha' stole her!"

CHAPTER IV

IN THE CAVE

"DID you git her?" whispered a hoarse, raucous voice.

"You bet we got her," responded the desperado as he and his two villainous looking companions lifted the swooning figure of Rosalie Spink from the sleigh and conducted her into the counterfeiters' cave in the cellar of the haunted house.

"See anything of the Hero on the way over?" demanded the woman, for such the first speaker was.

"No," growled the man, throwing Rosalie down in the damp corner. "I guess the plot's been changed. Dang it! What's he keepin' us waitin' for?" he snarled. "I want what's comin' to me quick."

"You'll get it all right," chuckled the hag.

"Give us a drink, mother — my ears is froze," put in the guttural voice of the second desperado, a tall, swart looking man with bloated cheeks.

"Hee-hee," laughed the hag, drunkenly, for she had been drinking. "Wait till the hero comes, my laddy-buck. He 'll give ye a rum punch that 'll warm ye."

"No more of that, dang ye!" snarled the man, "Ye may be my mother, woman, but that 's naught to me. I never picked ye out with that face."

"A-a-a-ah!" sneered Maude, angrily. "Since ye seen that gal's face ye think mine ain't a pretty one, eh? Say another word, Dave Juggins, and I 'll spile it!"

Rosalie shuddered at the hag's terrible threat. With her face spoiled what would become of the cover? And the hero had not seen her yet, either. The situation was becoming intolerable.

CHAPTER V

THE RESCUE

"BIFF!"
It was Wicker Basket's fist that broke thus upon the stillness of the night. The young son of Congressman Basket had fallen through the trap-door in the floor of the haunted house above where he had been spending the night, landing upon the stomach of the villain answering to the name of Sam, thereby putting Sam forever out of commission. With a savage oath Dave had sprung forward to seize the intruder by the throat, but Wicker Basket was not the hero of our story for nothing. With his right fist suddenly outstretched he pushed Dave's nose through the purlieus of his cerebellum, until it stuck out like a collar button on the back of his neck, at the same time grasping Bill, the third kidnapper, by the ankle with his left hand and flinging him up against the

wall with such force that he fell a senseless clod to the dank earth.

"My turn next!" cried the hag, with a murderous glance at Wicker, crouching like a cornered wildcat.

"Yes," panted Wicker. "And you are the toughest job of the four. I'll give you eight dollars, madam, if you'll hang yourself like a lady, three chapters ahead of time, and save us all a lot of unnecessary trouble."

This appeal to her cupidity was too much for the woman.

"Done!" she cried, and in a moment she was dangling from the end of a guy rope which Wicker had politely flung over a floor beam overhead to save her the exertion, with the eight dollars clutched avariciously in her hand.

Tenderly removing the money from the dead woman's fingers and replacing it in his pocket, Wicker Basket lifted Rosalie in his strong, loverly arms.

CHAPTER VI

IN THE SIGHT OF HEAVEN

"WHERE am I?" faintly gasped Rosalie, without opening her eyes.

"In my arms, sweetheart," replied Wicker tenderly.

"And you?" interrogatively murmured the girl.

"I am the hero you have been waiting for through all these weary pages — I mean ages," Wicker confessed.

Rosalie sighed softly and peeped at him out of the corner of her eye.

"And the story, then, is finished? I am so glad," she whispered, snuggling closer.

"No dear," said Wicker gloomily; "it ought to stop here, but I regret to say that there are still 138 pages of it yet to run."

"Oh, Wicker, must we go through it all? Is there no escape?" she pouted.

"Yes, darling!" he cried, passionately folding her to his breast. "In the sight of heaven you are already my wife. Let the story end here and now."

"But my income," began Rosalie.

"Your two dollars a year that these dead rascals here sought to make their own are now mine," said the young man; "but," he added in noble renunciation, "I will not keep them. They shall be settled on Daddy Jay!"

"And we shall live on what, Wicker?" asked Rosalie.

"Have no fear, beloved, I am rich. Father is a member of Congress," said Wicker Basket.

And the stepdaughter of Peterson Jay at that moment entered life's motor with Wicker Basket, and up to the hour of going to press was still speeding along the road to happiness in utter and blissful carelessness of 136 unlived pages of her subsequent history.

CHAPTER VII

CONCLUSION

WHO's darter was she, anyhow, Peterson?" asked Alf Boozeling one morning two years later as he and the retired town marshal met on the Post Office steps.

"I dunno yit," replied Peterson Jay. "I 've read the book through three times and I ain't quite sure as to the lady's identity afore she come, and none of the alleged folks in the Social Registry of New York, Bosting or Philadelphy ain't claimed her, but I tell ye, Alf, they 's one thing that 's derned cartain."

"What 's that, Peterson?" asked the Tankletown drunkard.

"So long as that there two dollars a year keeps comin' along good and reg'lar she 's welcome to call herself the stepdarter of Peterson Jay, by Heck!" said the old man proudly.

SOMEHOW LONG

By THE AUTHOR OF ALICE IN WANDERLAND

CHAPTER I

A MAN IN A BILLYCOCK HAT — THE MISSING
REMITTANCE — STILL MISSING — STRANGE
USE FOR A PAIR OF COUPONS SCISSORS —
THE PLOT THICKENS TUPPENCE WORTH

AN EXCEPTIONALLY well built man in green knickerbockers and tan shoes, wearing a billycock hat of the vintage of 1895, walked into the bank in the City and inquired if a credit had come for him by wireless from New York. The clerk would see. Come back in a week. This quite suited his purpose, for he had never seen the Tower of London, or visited Madame Tussaud's Wax Works, and, besides, that week's leeway would fill considerable space when it came to providing copy for the printer in the novel of which all unconsciously he was acting as the hero, for, mind you, it is not at all an easy task these days to write a novel five hundred and sixty-five pages, in solid small pica type, running not less than six hundred and forty-eight words to the page, without employing annoying little delays of this kind, making intervals which can be filled with extracts from the diary of the individual most concerned. Moreover, in no other way could Madame Tussaud's Wax Works, or the Tower either for that matter, which have nothing whatever to do with the story, be got into it, and so the man with the billycock hat, was quite willing to be put off in so light a matter as one involving a possible credit from New York, which in the end, even if it did arrive, by the time the voucher got back to New York, might not be worth the air it had taken to carry it across the Atlantic in days like these, when the air itself is full of the flying particles of bursted trust companies awaiting reorganisation.

"Has that credit come yet?" he inquired two weeks later, again addressing the young clerk at the bank, who wore a green necktie and sat behind the counter trimming the fringe off a pair of navy blue cuffs with a coupon scissors — not that this incident has anything whatever to do with the story, and we do not ourselves know why we have mentioned it, except because the idea entered our mind at the time we were penning this paragraph.

"Yes," said the young man, glancing furtively out of the window at a bobolink that was whistling the "Merry Widow" waltz while trying to balance himself on one of the Postal Union Telegraph poles that stood on that side of Cornhill; "yes, the credit has arrived, but the signature is coming by mail and will not be here until next Chuesday." Why young bank clerks call it Chuesday I do not know unless it be, as one of the editors of *Punch* once remarked, when asked to explain this singular habit, "because they chues to."

"All right," said the visitor. "That will give me time to buy a bottle of eau de Cologne and take a ride in the tuppenny tube as far as the British Museum, where they have a few liver mummies than you are on exhibition."

He went down the steps of the bank and on to the fate that awaited him.

CHAPTER II

TUBING — A NICE GIRL ENTERS — BUT SHE IS
A FALSE ALARM — A BARGAIN IS STRUCK —
A FAMILIAR NAME — AN ELECTRIC BELTRO-
CUTION

WHEN he had paid his fare in the tuppenny tube he had only thrippence left, but he was fascinated by the thought that that would enable him to ride back when the end of his outward journey had been reached, and he sat back in his cushioned seat and looked out upon the scenery in the tunnel, wondering in his mind whether or not he should get off at Tottenham Court Road or go on to the terminus. He would get more for his money if he went on to the terminus, but then he might not get back before next Chuesday.

What little things life sometimes hangs on! If he had got off at Tottenham Court Road his toe would not have been stepped on by his

113

divorced wife's daughter, and the rest of this entertaining story would have been up against it for subject matter. For at the next station beyond a girl got into the carriage, who might at first thought have passed for the main lady heroine of the story, but of that we shall hear anon. In passing him she stepped on his pet corn, and he winced visibly; but he forgave her, for she was a nice girl, and it was quite evident that she had not done it on purpose, as indeed how could she, never having seen him before, and therefore being entirely unaware that he had such a thing? Her apologies, profusely spread over some six or eight stations, naturally opened up opportunities for subsequent conversation, of which they both made the most. The girl, noting that he wore an electric belt around the outside of his waistcoat, remarked upon it.

"Do you think they are any good?" she asked.

"It depends on what you use them for," he said. "For imaginary rheumatism I think they are first rate, but they make poor watch chains."

"I only asked because I thought of getting

one for mother for a Christmas present," she said. "Are they expensive?"

"You can have this one for sixpence," he answered.

"Done," said she, tossing him a Canadian quarter.

"I have no change," said he.

"Send it to me by mail, in stamps" she replied. "There is my address."

She handed him a card, which he read:

MRS. FARTHINGALE

MISS DESDEMONA FARTHINGALE

NABISCOA VILLA, THIRD BELL

"I 'm not my mother," said the girl.

"But you are your mother's daughter," he inquired.

"I believe so," she replied, "though you never can tell. I believe ma got me and the alimony, though I never read the decree,"

"I 've heard the name before." said he, reaching down to the floor to pick up the Canadian quarter, which he had failed to catch when she tossed it to him.

"Look out there!" cried the guard, who

came along at this moment. "Your electric belt is slipping up over your neck, and it's against the rules of this company for travellers to be injured on these cars."

But it was too late. The electric belt had slipped upward as its owner bent downward, and the man sat there quite still and fixed.

"Have you got it?" asked the girl.

But the man spoke never a word. She had been a witness of an electric beltrocution!

CHAPTER III

MRS. FARTHINGALE — THE CAB AT THE DOOR — DR. JERRIKER — OMITTED HISTORY — A YOUNG DIVORCÉE — BY MAIL FROM SOUTH DAKOTA — DESDY PLEADS FOR THE HERO — MRS. FARTHINGALE PEEPS INTO THE CAB — SHE CHANGES HER MIND

WHAT is it, doctor?" asked Mrs. Farthingale as the cab drew up at the door of Nabiscoa Villa. (There's a ten page story, by the way, in how the villa came to have that name, involving the painter who whitewashed the original name of Ballston Spa off the gatepost and when ordered to restore it mixed too much alcohol with his pigments, which we would tell you if our slices were larger.)

"Nothing, Mrs. Farthingale," said Jerriker, "nothing at all — only — well, Desdy has brought home an interesting character in a modern novel who has had his memory

117

shocked out of him by wearing an electric belt on his neck."

"Mercy!" cried Mrs. Farthingale. "What on earth is she going to do with him?"

"There are some cases I can't diagnose, madam," said the doctor, shaking his head mournfully. "All I can say is that he is too heavy to hang on a Christmas tree."

"What is his name?" asked Mrs. Farthingale.

"He's forgotten it," said the doctor. "In fact, he has forgotten everything except his rather unusual knowledge of languages — even his address and the name of his bankers have gone completely from his memory. I don't believe he will ever remember my bill when I send it in."

Miss Farthingale's mother was still young and beautiful in spite of the fact that she had been a divorcée for twenty years. (Eighteen years of the lady's history is here omitted, although it is in the main perfectly proper reading for the young.) Nevertheless, she still loved her lost husband with all the passionate ardour of youth, and if he had only known that she had been guilty at the worst of a faux pas, and not of lèse majesté, which he would have known if he had listened to her when she tried to explain, instead of running away in a rage and sending her a South Dakota divorce by mail, she felt sure he would have forgiven her.

"You can't keep him, Desdykins," she remonstrated with her daughter. "You know as well as I do that our spare room is rented on alternate Thursdays to the Major."

"Oh, but, mamma, if it had n't been for my treading on his foot the electric belt never would have hit him in the neck," pleaded the girl. "Just look at him once, dear, and I am sure you will let him stay."

The cab was still standing at the curb, and Mrs. Farthingale's womanly curiosity prevailed. She walked to the cab window and looked in. A strange pallor came upon her face as she turned away. "He looks good to me, Desdy," she said. "You may carry him into the house."

CHAPTER IV

A WISE OLD MAJOR — ANYBODY LOST A HUS-
BAND AND FATHER? — IN THE GARDEN —
"DO YOU REMEMBER?" — ALGERNON REN-
WICK'S SHIRT — WHOSE WAS IT? — A HY-
MENEAL ENCORE

HE REMAINED that night at the house, but the next day remembered nothing, not even that he had remained that night at the house, but the Major had an observing eye.

"Look out for the stranger, Desdy," he said, as the young girl poured his tea one evening two weeks later. "That is, unless you want a stepfather."

"Well, why not?" answered Desdy, with a decided gollop in her eye, for to her her mother was perfection. "If mamma wants a step-husband, why should n't she have him? Here's hoping her luck will change, though — we 've had one chump in the family already."

"Yes, but who knows that the great unknown has n't a wife and eleven children already, and has forgotten them along with his name and address?" suggested the Major, pouring his toddy into the tea.

"We 've advertised him in the lost and found columns of the American and English newspapers for two solid weeks," replied Desdy with spirit. "If a family of that size cannot find a missing husband and father after all that they deserve to lose him."

Meanwhile Mrs. Farthingale was walking in the garden with the stranger.

"You still remember nothing?" she said.

"Nothing," he replied.

"Well, that 's something," said she, with a sight of relief. It was grasping nettles, but she nevertheless continued, for she was a strong woman. "You don't recall that twenty years ago, as Gerry Galliser, you married me, and two weeks later, because of some slight ante-nuptial indiscretions, for which I was not at all to blame, with Colonel Benderfield, under the chaperonage of his wife, you flew into a rage, cast me off, disappeared, got a divorce through some correspondence school in America, and sent it to me by mail?"

"Is this true?" he asked.

"Absolutely," she confessed. Oh, indeed she was a strong woman.

"Well, I hope I never hear of it," said he. "I don't remember anything of the kind, and I don't want to remember anything of the kind. I'm satisfied with things as they are. You have a comfortable home, a fair income — if I can judge by appearances — and a good cook. What else can a man want?"

"But the immediate past——"

"Let it stay forgotten," he answered. "When I think of all the tailor's bills, grocery bills, unpaid club charges and other unliquidated affairs that I have forgotten since that electric belt rose up and belted me, I wouldn't go back to the old life for a farm."

"Suppose you should change your mind? Suppose somebody should tell you that Desdy is not your daughter, and never was your daughter, what then?" she persisted, still grasping carpet tacks, for she was getting stronger every minute.

"She 'd be my stepdaughter," he replied. "That would be a step farther toward ——"

"Enough! I will be your wife again, Algernon!" she cried, throwing away the nettles and grasping him instead.

"Algernon?" he murmured dreamily, as he lifted his fiancée off his chest.

"Yes, dear," she whispered, for the moon had come out and she was afraid the occupants of the first and second floor back would hear. "You have got to have a name of some sort to get married with, and the name embroidered on your only shirt, which came back from the laundry yesterday, is Algernon Renwick."

"It 's as good as another," he said, pushing his fingers into his eyes, and striving to recall, but without avail, from whom he had borrowed the shirt.

And the next month Algernon Renwick was the name under which the stranger married Rosalind Farthingale.

How strange indeed are the things that fortune brings to pass! Here was a man married a second time to his first wife, whom he had divorced twenty years before, living under an assumed name, with apparently no other resources than the alimony paid to his second wife by her first husband! Think it over.

CHAPTER V

RECOGNITIONS — MORE RECOGNITIONS — REC-
OGNISED AGAIN — AT SONNENBERG — MR.
THOMSON — COLONEL ROBINSON — SEVERAL
OTHERS — IDENTIFIED — HOMEWARD BOUND

THEY were coming out of the Cathedral
at Rheims, and Renwick was deeply
thoughtful. So was Mrs. Renwick. The
first cloud had appeared to dim the glory of
her honeymoon. Renwick had been
addressed three times on their way to mass
by persons pretending to know him. The
plot was getting uncomfortably thick for
both of them, for each time he had been
called by a different name — Garrison, Jem-
mison, and Smitherson — but always Algernon; and the lady with the bronze hair and
Fluffy Ruffles hat had called him Jerry, not
Gerry, but Jerry, which showed what kind of
a person she was!

They arrived at Sonnenberg. You know

the great hotel, or pension, up near the Keeleyberg, that looks down on the lake, where William Tell shot the arrow — or the apple — or what was it he shot? If you don't know it does n't matter. We only mention it to fill out the page. What does matter is that here again was Renwick recognised — first by the fat Baron von Katzenjammer, who addressed him as Mr. Robinson, and asked him if he had ever returned Renwick's shirt! Then by an American tourist, who slapped him familiarly on the back with a cheerful "Hullo, Thomson, old man! How 's the wife and babies?" And the very next night at the concert at the Kursaal four different groups, all of them lively, sitting about the tables, also recognised him as he entered and simultaneously called to him to come and join them — only none of them used the same name, Tompkins, Wilkins, Bosbyshell, and Jinks, and, what was worse in every instance, he was now become Algy!

"I don't wonder you can't remember your name, Algernon," said Rosalind as they left next day for Nabiscoa Villa to escape further recognition, if indeed escape were possible. "It would be a superhuman task. I think, however, I have solved the mystery of your parentage."

"Have you, love?" Renwick replied, pressing her hand affectionately.

"Yes, dear," she answered softly. "I think your father was the City Directory."

"And my mother?" he cried.

"The Telephone Book, dearest. Your names suggest an alliance of that sort."

CHAPTER VI

BACK AT NABISCOA — MISGIVINGS — AN IN-
QUIRY — SOMEHOW LONG — A PROPOSAL —
PAST FOR PAST — THE END

RENWICK was glad to be back at Nabiscoa Villa, where he could be Renwick
without any interruption. He had grown
distinctly tired of being so many other people,
and to say the truth it was beginning to wear
somewhat on the nerves of Rosalind also.
The latter was constantly oppressed, too, by
the fear that the gossip about her own past —
for the Major had invited Renwick to the
Hari-Kari Club, where they never talked about
anything else but Mrs. Farthingale's indis-
cretion of twenty years ago — might reawaken
those terrible memories which had now lain
dormant for so long a time. If she lost her
husband a second time, what would life hold
for her? How could she escape the charge
that would surely be brought against her that

128

she was a very careless woman? And what judge in the event of another divorce would give her a second allowance of alimony from the same husband, even though she should set up the plea of contributory negligence in her defence? Poor Rosalind — she was still hugging those nettles! But even in the midst of our deepest trials, the bright sun has a way of bursting suddenly over all, and clearing away the shadows! The end was at hand, and it was a happy one, for one evening as they again paced the garden together while Desdy and the Major had gone to the theatre to see "Too Much Algernon," the reigning London farce of the season, Renwick spoke to her.

"Rosalind, my love," he said tenderly, "how near the end of this story are we?"

"We 've got as far as page 202, dearest," she answered. "There are 363 pages more."

"Merciful heavens!" he cried. "It 's Somehow Long is n't it?"

"Yes," she sighed. "This suspense is killing me. I am so afraid you will remember the things that I have told you about my past life."

"That is what I was going to speak about, my sweet," said he. "It's not killing me, because I am not an easy dier — no man who lives after he has been electric beltrocuted is apt to succumb to a mere literary strain of this sort — but it is giving me a bad headache every morning trying to keep up this everlasting forgetfulness. I have to remember to forget a lot of things I never can forget, and the effort is giving me paresis. Wherefore I say let us chuck it. There's no money in the job for us."

"I have n't seen any," she responded languidly, fearing what was coming. Did he remember after all, and was this the beginning of the end, or only the end of the beginning? Ah, who can tell?

"Now it seems to me, my darling," Renwick went on, "that a man with as many aliases as I seem to have must naturally be possessed of a pretty variegated past."

"Quite so," she answered pallidly.

"On the other hand, your past also has checkers on it, sweetheart," he continued dreamily. "From what I heard at the Hari-Kari Club yesterday, from everybody but the waiters and the cook, combined with what you have told me yourself, I judge that when it comes to past performances we 're neither of us in a position to offer odds to the other. Not much choice between us, eh ?"

"Not any too much," she replied, her heart beating fast.

"Well then, let 's begin fresh. I 'll match my past against yours, and you can match yours against mine. I don't want to go back to those forgotten tailor's bills and you don't want to get your name in the papers again in connection with the South Dakota courts. Let 's forget we ever had any pasts at all or ever agreed to go through those remaining pages of Somehow Long. Eh ?"

She looked over the wall at the rising moon.

"But how about the author, Gerry ?" she asked softly. "Is it fair to leave him in the lurch ?"

"He can fill up on Desdy and Jerriker." Renwick replied. "If they are n't enough he can buy a Baedeker and introduce that into his novel, or enter upon a discussion of the relative value of tomato ketchup and chutney sauce as aids to the digestion of crab meat. It won't be the first time that he has introduced irrelevant matter into his stories, and it will leave us to the enjoyment of our alimony together."

Our alimony! How sweet it was to hear!

.   .   .   .

And they went next morning to the bank together to collect it.

Reprint Publishing

FOR PEOPLE WHO GO FOR ORIGINALS.

This book is a facsimile reprint of the original edition. The term refers to the facsimile with an original in size and design exactly matching simulation as photographic or scanned reproduction.

Facsimile editions offer us the chance to join in the library of historical, cultural and scientific history of mankind, and to rediscover.

The books of the facsimile edition may have marks, notations and other marginalia and pages with errors contained in the original volume. These traces of the past refers to the historical journey that has covered the book.

ISBN 978-3-95940-067-1

Facsimile reprint of the original edition
Copyright © 2015 Reprint Publishing
All rights reserved.

www.reprintpublishing.com

www.ingramcontent.com/pod-product-compliance
Lightning Source LLC
Chambersburg PA
CBHW071349170626
46811CB00003B/1056